# The Story of
# Little Black Sambo

## Helen Bannerman

Helen Bannerman

Filiquarian Publishing, LLC is publishing this edition of The Story of Little Black Sambo, due to its public domain status.

The cover design of this edition of The Story of Little Black Sambo is copyright 2007, Filiquarian Publishing, LLC.

Filiquarian Publishing, LLC

# Contents

**Helen Bannerman**

# The Story of Little Black Sambo

# Preface

There is very little to say about the story of Little Black Sambo. Once upon a time there was an English lady in India, where black children abound and tigers are everyday affairs, who had two little girls. To amuse these little girls she used now and then to invent stories, for which, being extremely talented, she also drew and coloured the pictures.

Among these stories Little Black Sambo, which was made up on a long railway journey, was the favourite; and it has been put into a dumpy book, and the pictures copies as exactly as possible, in the hope that you will like it as much as the two little girls did.

# LITTLE BLACK SAMBO

**O**nce upon a time there was a little black boy, and his name was Little Black Sambo.

7

## And his mother was called Black Mumbo.

## And his father was called Black Jumbo.

**And Black Mumbo made him a beautiful little Red Coat, and a pair of beautiful little blue trousers.**

And Black Jumbo went to the Bazaar, and bought him a beautiful Green Umbrella, and a lovely little Pair of Purple Shoes with Crimson Soles and Crimson Linings.

And then wasn't Little Black Sambo grand?

So he put on all his Fine Clothes, and went out for a walk in the Jungle.

And by and by he met a Tiger. And the Tiger said to him, "Little Black Sambo, I'm going to eat you up!" And Little Black Sambo said, "Oh! Please Mr. Tiger, don't eat me up, and I'll give you my beautiful little Red Coat." So the Tiger said, "Very well, I won't eat you this time, but you must give me your beautiful little Red Coat." So the Tiger got poor Little Black Sambo's beautiful little Red

Coat, and went away saying, "Now I'm the grandest Tiger in the Jungle."

And Little Black Sambo went on, and by and by he met another Tiger, and it said to him, "Little Black Sambo, I'm going to eat you up!"

And Little Black Sambo said, "Oh! Please Mr. Tiger, don't eat me up, and I'll give you my beautiful little Blue Trousers." So the Tiger said, "Very well, I won't eat you this time, but you must give me your beautiful little Blue Trousers." So the Tiger got poor Little Black Sambo's beautiful little Blue Trousers, and went away saying, "Now I'm the grandest Tiger in the Jungle."

And Little Black Sambo went on, and by and by he met another Tiger, and it said to him, "Little Black Sambo, I'm going to eat you up!" And Little Black Sambo said, "Oh! Please Mr. Tiger, don't eat me up, and I'll give you my beautiful little Purple Shoes with Crimson Soles and Crimson Linings."

15

But the Tiger said, "What use would your shoes be to me? I've got four feet, and you've got only two; you haven't got enough shoes for me."

But Little Black Sambo said, "You could wear them on your ears."

"So I could," said the Tiger: "that's a very good idea. Give them to me, and I won't eat you this time."

So the Tiger got poor Little Black Sambo's beautiful little Purple Shoes with Crimson Soles and Crimson Linings, and went away saying, "Now I'm the grandest Tiger in the Jungle."

And by and by Little Black Sambo met another
Tiger, and it said to him, "Little Black Sambo, I'm
going to eat you up!"

And Little Black Sambo said, "Oh! Please Mr.
Tiger, don't eat me up, and I'll give you my
beautiful Green Umbrella." But the Tiger said,
"How can I carry an umbrella, when I need all my
paws for walking with?"

"You could tie a knot on your tail and carry it that
way," said Little Black Sambo. "So I could," said
the Tiger." Give it to me, and I won't eat you this
time." So he got poor Little Black Sambo's
beautiful Green Umbrella, and went away saying,
"Now I'm the grandest Tiger in the Jungle."

And poor Little Black Sambo went away crying,
because the cruel Tigers had taken all his fine
clothes.

Presently he heard a horrible noise that sounded like "Gr-r-r- r-rrrrr," and it got louder and louder. "Oh! dear!" said Little Black Sambo, "there are all the Tigers coming back to eat me up! What shall I do?" So he ran quickly to a palm-tree, and peeped round it to see what the matter was.

And there he saw all the Tigers fighting, and disputing which of them was the grandest. And at last they all got so angry that they jumped up and took off all the fine clothes, and began to tear each other with their claws, and bite each other with their great big white teeth.

And they came, rolling and tumbling right to the foot of the very tree where Little Black Sambo was hiding, but he jumped quickly in behind the umbrella. And the Tigers all caught hold of each other's tails, as they wrangled and scrambled, and so they found themselves in a ring round the tree.

Then, when the Tigers were very wee and very far away, Little Black Sambo jumped up, and called out, "Oh! Tigers! why have you taken off all your nice clothes? Don't you want them any more?" But the Tigers only answered, "Gr-r-rrrr!"

Then Little Black Sambo said, "If you want them, say so, or I'll take them away." But the Tigers would not let go of each other's tails, and so they could only say "Gr-r-r-rrrrrr!"

So Little Black Sambo put on all his fine clothes again and walked off.

And the Tigers were very, very angry, but still they would not let go of each other's tails. And they were so angry, that they ran round the tree, trying to eat each other up, and they ran faster and faster, till they were whirling round so fast that you couldn't see their legs at all.

And they still ran faster and faster and faster, till they all just melted away, and there was nothing left but a great big pool of melted butter (or "ghi," as it is called in India) round the foot of the tree.

Now Black Jumbo was just coming home from his work, with a great big brass pot in his arms, and when he saw what was left of all the Tigers he said, "Oh! what lovely melted butter! I'll take that home to Black Mumbo for her to cook with."

So he put it all into the great big brass pot, and took it home to Black Mumbo to cook with.

When Black Mumbo saw the melted butter, wasn't she pleased! "Now," said she, "we'll all have pancakes for supper!"

So she got flour and eggs and milk and sugar and butter, and she made a huge big plate of most lovely pancakes. And she fried them in the melted butter which the Tigers had made, and they were just as yellow and brown as little Tigers.

And then they all sat down to supper. And Black Mumbo ate Twenty-seven pancakes, and Black Jumbo ate Fifty-five but Little Black Sambo ate a Hundred and Sixty-nine, because he was so hungry.

# The Story of Little Black Mingo

Once upon a time there was a little black girl, and her name was **Little Black Mingo.**

She had no father and mother, so she had to live with a horrid cross old woman called **Black Noggy,** who used to scold her every day, and sometimes beat her with a stick, even though she had done nothing naughty.

29

One day Black Noggy called her, and said,

"Take this chatty {ed. A chatty is a large ceramic vase used to carry water.} down to the river and fill it with water, and come back as fast as you can, QUICK NOW!"

So Little Black Mingo took the chatty and ran down to the river as fast as she could, and began to fill it with water, when Cr-r-rrrack!!! Bang!!! A horrible big Mugger {ed. A Mugger is an alligator like creature.} poked its nose up through the bottom of the chatty and said "Ha, ha!! Little Mingo, I'm going to eat you up!"

Little Black Mingo did not say anything. She turned and ran away as fast as ever she could, and the Mugger ran after her. But the broken chatty round his neck caught his paws, so he could not overtake her.

31

But when she got back to Black Noggy, and told her how the Mugger had broken the chatty, Black Noggy was fearfully angry. "You naughty girl," she said, "you have broken the chatty yourself, I have a good mind to beat you." And if she had not been in such a hurry for the water she WOULD have beaten her.

Then she went and fetched the great big chatty that the dhobi used to boil the clothes in. "Take this," said she, "and mind you don't break it, or I WILL beat you."

"But I can't carry that when it is full of water," said Little Black Mingo.

"You must go twice, and bring it half full each time," said Black Noggy.

So Little Black Mingo took the dhobi's great big chatty, and started again to go to the river. But first she went to a little bank above the river, and peeped up and down, to see if she could see the old Mugger anywhere. But she could not see him, for he was hiding under the very bank she was standing on, and though his tail stuck out a little she never saw him at all.

She would have liked to run home, but she was too much afraid that Black Noggy would beat her.

So Little Black Mingo crept down to the river, and began to fill the big chatty with water. And while she was filling it the Mugger came creeping softly down behind her and caught her by the tail, saying, "Aha, Little Black Mingo, now I've got you."

And Little Black Mingo said, "Oh! Please don't eat me up, great big Mugger."

"What will you give me, if I don't eat you up?" said the Mugger. But Little Black Mingo was so poor she had nothing to give. So the Mugger caught her in his great cruel mouth and swam

35

away with her to an island in the middle of the river and set her down beside a huge pile of eggs.

"Those are my eggs," said he; "to-morrow a little mugger will come out of each, and then we will have a great feast, and we will eat you up."

Then he waddled off to catch fish for himself, and left Little Black Mingo alone beside the big pile of eggs.

And Little Black Mingo sat down on a big stone and hid her face in her hands, and cried bitterly, because she couldn't swim and she didn't know how to get away.

36

Presently she heard a queer little squeaky noise that sounded like "Squeak, Squeak, Squeak!!! Oh Little Black Mingo, help me or I shall be drowned." She got up and looked to see what was calling, and she saw a bush coming floating down the river with something wriggling and scrambling about in it, and as it came near she saw that it was a Mongoose that was in the bush. So she waded out as far as she could, and caught hold of the bush and pulled it in, and the poor Mongoose crawled up her arm on to her shoulder, and she carried him to shore.

When they got to shore the Mongoose shook himself, and Little Black Mingo wrung out her petticoat, and so they both very soon got dry.

The Mongoose then began to poke about for something to eat, and very soon he found the great big pile of Mugger's eggs. "Oh, joy!" said he, "what's this?"

"Those are Mugger's eggs," said Little Black Mingo.

"I'm not afraid of Muggers!" said the Mongoose; and he sat down and began to crack the eggs, and eat the little muggers as they came out. And he threw the shells into the water, so that the old Mugger should not see that any one had been eating them. But he was careless, and he left one eggshell on the edge, and he was hungry and he ate so many that the pile got much smaller, and when the old Mugger came back he saw at once that some one had been meddling with them.

So he ran to Little Black Mingo, and said, "How dare you eat my eggs?, "Indeed, indeed I didn't," said Little Black Mingo., "Then who could it have been?" said the Mugger, and he ran back to the eggs as fast as he could, and sure enough when he got back he found the Mongoose had eaten a whole lot more!!

39

Then he said to himself, "I must stay beside my eggs till they are hatched into little muggers, or the Mongoose will eat them all." So he curled himself into a ring round the eggs and went to sleep.

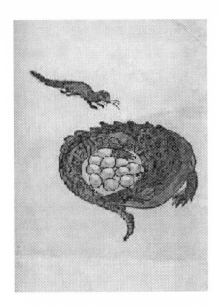

But while he was asleep the Mongoose came to eat some more of the eggs, and ate as many as he wanted, and when the Mugger woke this time, oh! What a rage he was in, for there were only six eggs left! He roared so loud that all the little muggers inside the shells gnashed their teeth, and tried to roar too.

Then he said, "I know what I'll do, I'll fetch Little Black Mingo's big chatty and cover my eggs with that, then the Mongoose won't be able to get at them." So he swam across to the shore, and fetched the dhobi's big chatty, and covered the eggs with it. "Now, you wicked little Mongoose, come and eat my eggs if you can," said he, and he went off quite proud and happy.

By and by the Mongoose came back, and he was terribly disappointed when he found the eggs all covered with the big chatty.

41

So he ran off to Little Black Mingo, and asked her to help him, and Little Black Mingo came and took the big chatty off the eggs, and the Mongoose ate them every one.

"Now," said he, "there will be no little muggers to make a feast for tomorrow."

"No," said Little Black Mingo, "but the Mugger will eat me all by himself I am afraid."

"No he won't," said the Mongoose, "for we will sail away together in the big chatty before he comes back."

So he climbed on to the edge of the chatty, and
Little Black Mingo pushed the chatty out into the
water, and then she clambered into it and paddled
with her two hands as hard as she could, and the
big chatty just sailed beautifully.

So they got across safely, and Little Black Mingo
filled the chatty half full of water and took it on
her head, and they went up the bank together.

But when the Mugger came back, and found only
empty egg- shells he was fearfully angry. He
roared and he raged, and he howled and he yelled,
till the whole island shook, and his tears ran down
his cheeks and pattered on the sand like rain.

So he started to chase Little Black Mingo and the Mongoose, and he swam across the river as fast as ever he could, and when he was half way across he saw them landing, and as he landed they hurried over the first ridge.

So he raced after them, but they ran, and just before he caught them they got into the house, and banged the door in his face. Then they shut all the windows, so he could not get in anywhere.

"All right," said he, "you will have to come out some time, and then I will catch you both, and eat you up."

So he hid behind the back of the house and waited.

Now Black Noggy was just coming home from the bazaar with a tin of kerosene on her head, and a box of matches in her hand.

And when he saw her the Mugger rushed out and gobbled her up, kerosene tin, matches and all!!!

When Black Noggy found herself in the Muggers' dark inside, she wanted to see where she was, so she felt for the match- box and took out a match and lit it. But the Mugger's teeth had made holes in the kerosene tin, so that the flame of the match

45

caught the kerosene, and BANG!! the kerosene exploded, and blew the old Mugger and Black Noggy into little bits.

At the fearful noise Little Black Mingo and the Mongoose came running out, and there they found Black Noggy and the old Mugger all blown to bits.

So Little Black Mingo and the Mongoose got the nice little house for their very own, and there they lived happy ever after. And Little Black Mingo got the Mugger's beard for her seat, and the Mongoose got Black Noggy's handkerchief for his. But he was so wee he used to put it on the Mugger's nose, and there they sat, and had their tea every evening.

LaVergne, TN USA
10 November 2010

204315LV00003B/210/A